TEDDY SCARES

CREEPING IT REAL
A *Fur-ociously* Fun Guidebook

by Sierra Harimann

Scholastic Inc.

ISBN 978-1-338-68050-8

10 9 8 7 6 5 4 3 2 1   20 21 22 23 24

Printed in the U.S.A.   40
First printing 2020
Designed by Cheung Tai

CONTENTS

Meet the Teddy Scares!

Awwww . . . how cute! Or *are* they? These cuddly terrors were once regular teddy bears. But when their owners outgrew them, they were thrown away. With no place else to go, the abandoned bears made a new home for themselves—at the trash dump.

Now these a*gore*able bears spend their time having fun, going on adventures, and getting into trouble! Though they all have different personalities, deep down, these furry freaks are all seeking the same thing: someone to love them enough to take them home.

The Dump

The trash dump the Teddy Scares live in is a strange place. At its heart is the Incinerator. The area around the Incinerator is active and busy during the day, and the bears avoid it if they can. But at night, they often head there on adventures. It's where they find the best junk, since it's where the newest trash ends up.

Beyond the Incinerator are the Trash Hills. These many mounds of garbage have built up over a long, long time. It will take years and years for the workers at the dump to get through it all.

MEET

Abnormal Cyrus

Unlike the other abandoned bears, Cyrus never had a chance to bond with his human owner. That's because his missing eye meant he was considered defective early in his life. He bounced around from yard sales to thrift stores to flea markets before he finally landed at the trash dump.

These days, Cyrus's one goal is to find a true best friend. In the meantime, this oddball bear marches to the beat of his own drum. He can be absentminded, but he has a warm, loving heart.

Abnormal Cyrus

Nickname: Cy

Best qualities: He's enthusiastic, easy-going, child-like, creative, and curious.

Unbearable traits: He's socially awkward, and a bit clumsy.

Favorite food: Cheesy brussels-sprout tacos

Favorite color: Any shade of green

Favorite hobbies: Drawing comics, riding his unicycle

Favorite saying: "If it isn't unique, what's the point?"

AS FUR AS I SEE IT,

WE'RE ALL A LITTLE WEIRD.

MEET
Rita Mortis

Before she landed at the dump, teddy bear Rita and her girl, Violet, were inseparable. But one day, bullies stole Violet's backpack. They tossed it into a dumpster with Rita inside! When she woke up, Rita was alone, without Violet, for the first time. She was terrified.

But Rita's fear quickly turned to anger. She had been taken from her best friend! Hardened by this separation, Rita vowed never to be afraid again. But her hard-as-steel exterior hides her soft, cuddly inside. The truth is, if Violet showed up at the dump, Rita would go home with her in a heartbeat.

For now, though, Rita is the unofficial leader of the bears. Redmond is her pranking buddy and the closest thing she has to a friend—not that she would ever admit to something so mushy.

Rita Mortis

Nickname: Wreck-It Rita

Best qualities: She's tough, mostly fearless, and independent.

Unbearable traits: She can be bossy.

Favorite food: Rare steaks

Favorite color: Bloodred

Favorite hobbies: Smashing trash for fun, running, playing pranks on the other bears

Favorite saying: "You got a problem with that?!"

MEET
Edwin Morose

Crushed by the loss of his one true love, Edwin arrived at the dump with a broken heart, and he's never fully recovered. Edwin has the soul of a tragic poet. On most days, he can be found jotting down bits of cheesy poetry for a nonexistent girlfriend or matching wits with his best friend, Hester.

But within this sad ball of fluff lives a part-time optimist. Some days, Edwin wanders the dump feeling hopeful, sure that he'll find peace—and true love—again.

Edwin Morose

Nickname: Ed

Best qualities: He's thoughtful, compassionate, sweet, and honest.

Unbearable traits: He can be clingy and glum.

Favorite food: Fruit dipped in chocolate fondue . . . for one

Favorite color: Blue

Favorite hobbies: Writing poetry and having long, meaningful conversations with his friend Hester

Favorite saying: "Just cry it out and you'll feel better."

I HATE TO BE THE BEARER OF SAD NEWS, BUT I CAN'T HELP IT.

MEET
Eli Wretch

Eli is a bit of a loner and would rather be tinkering with a project than hanging out with the other bears. This master engineer is incredibly resourceful. He can build just about anything with what he finds at the dump.

Eli's extroverted side comes out when one of the other bears has a project of their own. Eli is the first to help—and his assistance always comes with loads of tips and advice. At times, Eli's wisdom leaves the other bears more confused than before. But deep down, he means well. Eli is almost as brilliant as Hester, though not in a book-smart kind of way.

Eli Wretch

Nickname: Mr. Fix-It

Best qualities: He's hardworking, clever, resourceful, and dependable.

Unbearable traits: He can be stubborn.

Favorite food: Meatloaf, pork chops, and fried chicken

Favorite color: Army green

Favorite hobbies: Tinkering away in his own private corner of the dump

Favorite saying: "I'll fix it even if it isn't broken."

HERE'S MY ADVICE:

JUST GRIN AND BEAR IT.

MEET
Mazey Podge

Mazey is a patchwork teddy bear and was created by a seamstress who assembled and reassembled her constantly, telling Mazey how perfect she was going to be. Even after her owner passed away, Mazey continued to believe in herself completely.

Mazey likes pretty things and pretty surroundings, which makes living at the dump hard for her at times. She's sweet and cute—and she knows how to use that to get her way. Rita can't stand Mazey's girliness, but the two bears have more in common than Rita realizes: Just like Rita, Mazey isn't going to let anyone get in the way of what she wants. And like the other bears, Mazey would love to find a new owner who could provide the fabulous lifestyle she knows she deserves.

Mazey Podge

Nickname: Maze

Best qualities: She's confident, fun-loving, optimistic, and spontaneous.

Unbearable traits: She's materialistic and can be manipulative.

Favorite food: Chocolate-covered strawberries

Favorite color: Pink—what else?

Favorite hobbies: Sewing, ballet, looking at herself in the mirror

Favorite saying: "How do I look?"

LIFE IS FULL

OF

PAWSIBILITIES

MEET

Redmond Gore

This silent bear wears a potato sack over his head. He's very insecure about his appearance, and he either can't or won't speak, though no one knows exactly why. But whenever he gets into a scrape in the dump, Redmond seems to have an almost magical ability to walk away unscathed.

Redmond is on the outskirts of the group, though he enjoys spending time with Rita. She and Reds (a nickname she came up with) like to wander the dump looking for trash to chop up for fun. Though he comes off as aloof and scary, deep down he cares. When push comes to shove, he would do anything to defend the other bears.

R.I.P.

Redmond Gore

Nickname: Reds

Best qualities: He's loyal, protective, and stealthy.

Unbearable traits: He can be aggressive and destructive.

Favorite food: Anything he can sip through a straw so he doesn't have to remove his potato sack

Favorite color: Brown

Favorite hobbies: Smashing and chopping up trash with Rita

Favorite saying: " . . . "

STRONG

SILENT TYPE

MEET
Hester Golem

Hester has no memory of his life before the dump, though he has pieced together a few details about his origins. He knows his brand of teddy bear was first produced in the 1880s, so he is well over one hundred years old. Thanks to his age and to the work of roaches, Hester has suffered from stuffing loss and memory loss over time.

Hester is an eloquent bear—he's the brains of the bunch. This bookworm loves to read, and he's a great problem solver. Hester shares a love of books and history with Edwin, his closest friend. Sometimes Hester can be a bit too impressed with his own intellect, though, which can rub the others the wrong way. Still, when a problem requires brains over brawn, the bears look to Hester.

Hester Golem

Nickname: Boss

Best qualities: He is brilliant, analytical, and detail-oriented.

Unbearable traits: He can be pompous, arrogant, and impatient.

Favorite food: Coffee, coffee, and more coffee

Favorite color: Royal blue

Favorite hobbies: Debating philosophy and history with Edwin

Favorite saying: "Every problem has a solution if you know where to look."

MEET

Sheldon Grogg

Before he landed at the dump, Sheldon led an ideal life with an owner who loved and cared for him. He arrived at the dump when his owner outgrew him. The happiness of his past life has stayed with Sheldon, and he has a peaceful, relaxed vibe and a healthy outlook on his new life.

Sheldon's main issue is with sleep at night: Without his owner to cuddle him, he suffers from insomnia. That means he often nods off at random times throughout the day. He usually gets along well with the other bears, but his frequent naps leave him open to Rita and Redmond's constant pranks.

Sheldon Grogg

Nickname: Shelly

Best qualities: He's calm, gentle, and patient.

Unbearable traits: He's shy, and liable to fall asleep in the middle of a sentence.

Favorite food: Chamomile tea and cookies

Favorite color: Sky blue

Favorite hobbies: Yawning, reading bedtime stories

Favorite saying: "Is it bedtime yet?"

MEET

Annabelle Wraithia

Annabelle's history is a sad one: Before she came to the dump, she was the bride in a bride-and-groom centerpiece at a wedding reception. After the party ended, she fell off the decoration and was left behind. Sadly, when she arrived at the dump, Annabelle became trapped in the Incinerator, where she perished.

Though her body was destroyed, her spirit lives on. Annabelle haunts the dump as a sweet and loving—but

sad—ghost. It isn't easy being trapped between two worlds, but Annabelle makes the best of it.

Annabelle Wraithia

Nickname: Anna

Best qualities: She is sweet, caring, and loving.

Unbearable traits: She can be depressing to be around.

Favorite food: Leftover wedding cake

Favorite color: White

Favorite hobbies: Ballroom dancing, dead flower arranging

Favorite saying: "To have and to hold, until death do us part."

ALWAYS THE BRIDESMAID BEAR, NEVER THE BRIDE.

MEET

Mundy Drudge

Mundy is the result of an experiment in Hester's makeshift lab. Over time, Hester gathered various fabric pieces and parts from around the dump and used them to create an entirely new bear. Then he used some of his own stuffing to fill him. The result is the Frankenbear, Mundy.

Mundy's unique design means he is incredibly durable, while his patchwork quality means he has many different sides to his personality. Sometimes he manages to stay cute and creepy, but other times, this teddy can be downright scary!

Mundy Drudge

Nickname: Frankie

Best qualities: He's strong, tough, and a master of dark comedy.

Unbearable traits: He's the most frightening bear in the bunch.

Favorite food: Fried rattlesnake

Favorite color: Black

Favorite hobbies: Writing horror stories

Favorite saying: "If I cannot inspire love, I will cause fear!"

MEET

Granger Evermore

This bear may look grizzly on the outside, but he has a heart of gold. Before he came to the trash dump, Granger was a novelty bear available for purchase at an old prison-turned-museum. After years spent sitting on the shelf, he wound up at the dump, never having found a human to love him.

Granger didn't mind his quiet, solitary life on the shelf, though. Even now, he prefers his own company to the company of the other bears. The exception is Granger's soft spot for those in need. He serves as the dump's unofficial security guard, and he's made it his mission to protect new arrivals from the dangers of the Incinerator.

Granger Evermore

Nickname: Maximum G

Best qualities: He's patient, and he has a strong conscience and a heart of gold.

Unbearable traits: He can be distant and cold at times.

Favorite food: Processed meat and instant noodles

Favorite color: Gray

Favorite hobbies: Shooting hoops with pieces of trash

Favorite saying: "Steer clear of the Incinerator!"

QUIZ:

Who is Your Spirit Bear?

Which of the Teddy Scares do you most relate to? Take this quiz to find out!

1. It's your best friend's birthday and you're looking for the perfect card. Which do you choose?

   A. Something sweet so my friend knows how much I care.

   B. A card? I don't need a mushy card to show my feelings.

   C. The weirdest, funniest card I can find! My friend gets my sense of humor.

   D. Something bright and fun, like a party on paper!

2. What is your favorite type of sport?

A. Something expressive *and* athletic, like ice skating.

B. Roller derby: The more intense the sport, the better.

C. A unique, individual sport like skateboarding.

D. A social, team sport, like soccer.

3. Which two colors do you prefer?

A. Yellow and lavender

B. Black and white

C. Orange and green

D. Teal and magenta

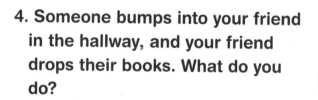

4. Someone bumps into your friend in the hallway, and your friend drops their books. What do you do?

A. Rush to your friend's aid, shouting dramatically for help.

B. Immediately go after the person who bumped your friend.

C. You were busy with your own thing and didn't even notice.

D. Help your friend up while offering an encouraging word.

5. Your favorite thing to do on the weekend is:

A. Listen to music while reading or writing in your journal.

B. Go for a long run.

C. Who knows? Probably something random and creative.

D. Hang out with friends, of course.

6. How would you best describe your style?

A. Preppy

B. Goth/punk

C. Unusual and mismatched

D. Fun and trendy

7. Which pet would you prefer?

A. A cat
B. A pet rock
C. A tarantula
D. A dog

8. What is your favorite genre of book or movie?

A. Romance
B. Horror
C. Adventure
D. Comedy

9. You need to make some spending money. What are you most likely to do?

A. Open your own lemonade or cupcake stand.

B. Shovel snow or do yardwork for the neighbors.

C. Create and sell your own artwork.

D. Start babysitting.

10. What's your favorite type of music?

A. Emo love songs

B. Punk

C. Indie rock

D. Pop

QUIZ RESULTS

Take a look back at all your answers and see which letter you chose the most. If there's no clear winner, you're likely an equal blend of all the bears' absolutely a*gore*able personality types!

Now turn the page to see which teddy is your spirit bear . . .

Mostly A: Edwin

If you chose mostly A's, yes, you *are* emo. Edwin is your spirit bear. You have a sensitive soul, and you're not afraid to show off your soft side. You're a kind and thoughtful friend, and you are always looking out for those around you.

Mostly B: Rita

Rebel with a CAUSE.

If you chose mostly B's, you're a rebel. Rita is your spirit bear. You're tough and you aren't afraid to do what's right. You always speak your mind and you're the first one to stand up for someone else. You're confident, strong, independent, and fearless.

Mostly C: Cyrus

Easily amused

If you chose mostly C's, you are a true original; Cyrus is your spirit bear. You are enthusiastic and easygoing, and you're bursting with creative ideas. You don't let anyone tell you what to do because you're too busy hatching your own unique plans.

Mostly D: Mazey

Stitched to perfection

If you chose mostly D's, you're the life of the party. Mazey is your spirit bear. You get your energy from being around other people. You want to be liked, and you crave attention. You know how to look on the bright side in any situation, and you're fun to be around.

Hester Golem's Build-a-Scare WORKSHOP

Mundy Drudge may be the original Frankenbear, but that hasn't stopped Hester from imagining his next clever creation. In fact, he may just give his friends makeovers one day. Here are some new combos he might try:

Abnormal Cyrus + a superhero =

Redmond Gore +
a ghost =

Mazey Podge + a vampire =

Sheldon Grogg +
a mummy =

Annabelle Wraithia + a unicorn =

Eli Wretch +
a race car driver =

Rita Mortis + a fairy godmother =

How the Teddy Bear Got Its Name

by Hester Golem

I may have some memory loss, but I will never forget this . . . The year was 1902, and United States President Theodore Roosevelt was invited on a bear-hunting trip in Mississippi by the state's governor. Roosevelt was well known as a big-game hunter, but on this trip, he didn't have any luck finding a bear. But some of the other hunters captured a bear and tied it to a tree. They then encouraged Roosevelt to shoot it, but the president refused, calling it unsportsmanlike behavior.

Newspapers around the country reported the event, and one political cartoonist, Clifford Berryman, decided to tease the president for refusing to shoot the bear. His cartoon ran in *The Washington Post* on November 16, 1902. A candy store owner in Brooklyn named Morris Michtom saw the cartoon. He and his wife, Rose, liked to make stuffed toy animals, and the cartoon gave Michtom an idea. The couple made a stuffed toy bear and put it on display in the candy shop's window. Michtom wrote to Roosevelt, and with the president's permission, he called his creation "Teddy's Bear."

From then on, we were teddy bears . . . and once abandoned, we became Teddy Scares!

TOP 20 REJECTED TEDDY SCARES NAMES

The teddy bear's name may be cute, but rest assured that you'll never meet one of the Teddy Scares at the trash dump with one of *these* names . . .

20. Fuzzy Wuzzy

19. Ted E. Bear

18. Huggie the Bear

17. Ms. Flufferberg

16. B.P. Cuddlesworth

15. Smooshy LaRoux

14. Sparkle Snugglepuss

13. Schmoopie Pie

12. Fluffer Nutter

11. Softy Sugarball

10. Mr. McMittens

9. Boo Boo Brambles

8. Mr. Squishie

7. Cuddly Poo

6. Tuffy Teddy

5. Sergeant Snuggles

4. Miss Kisses

3. Fluffy McFlufferson

2. Captain Cuddles

And the #1 most-rejected name is . . .

1. Sir Snuggles-a-lot

Hester Golem's Top Five Favorite

BOOKS

5. *The Great Grizzly*
   by F. Scott Fitzgerald

4. *Fur Whom the Bear Tolls*
   by Ernest Hemingway

3. *Frankenbear*
   by Mary Shelley

2. *A Tail of Two Teddies*
   by Charles Dickens

1. *Hairy Pawter and the Sorcerer's Stone*
   by J.K. Growling

Abnormal Cyrus's Top Ten

TRASH CREATIONS

Poor Cyrus is always on the lookout for a true best friend. Sometimes he gets so lonely at the dump, he creates new creatures out of trash to hang out with. Here are his top ten favorite finds-turned-friends:

10. **Creepy Clam: A plastic salad clamshell with rusty nails for eyes.**

9. **Roach Roll: A giant cockroach made out of cardboard toilet paper and paper towel rolls.**

8. **Corky: This creepy, crawly spider was crafted out of a used cork.**

7. **Jelly Jar: A jellyfish made out of a broken jam jar and some fairy lights.**

6. **Pizza Face:** This creature has a greasy, gross pizza box for a face.

5. **Junkbot:** This robot is made from various old car parts and toys.

4. **The Chained Spirit:** A ghost made from an old bedsheet wrapped in chains made from soda can tabs.

3. **Trash Kraken:** An enormous monster with tentacles made from pieces of plastic trash.

2. **Pitchfork Brain:** This plastic fork got a makeover, and now he's quite a fright.

1. **Eyeball:** This monster made out of an old tennis ball has one eye . . . and that's it!

Eli Wretch's
BAD ADVICE

The quietly quirky Eli loves giving the other Teddy Scares lots of advice. Unfortunately, his advice isn't always so great.

Eli's Top Five Bits of "Advice":

5. "A good bear giving bad advice is better than a bad bear giving good advice."

4. "Don't ask for advice if you don't want to hear it."

3. "If you can tell that someone's giving you bad advice, good for you."

2. "Never miss a chance to tell someone what you *really* think."

1. "Your head's already stuffed with fluff—why not add a little more?"

Things NOT to Say Around Annabelle Wraithia

"Oh this? It's just my diamond engagement ring from the famous store De Bears. You know, because diamonds are *fur*ever."

"Have you seen the movie *My Bear Friend's Wedding*?"

"That detail was like the icing on the cake . . ."

"They lived happily ever after . . ."

"Did you fall in love— or did you fall off the cake?"

Edwin Morose's
FAVORITE POEMS

Roses are red,

Violets are blue,

I feel so lost

When I'm without you.

Jack and Jill
Went up the trash hill
To see what was upon it.
They found a crown,
All rusty and brown,
And fought over who would wear it.

Are you sleeping,
Are you sleeping,
Sheldon Grogg? Sheldon Grogg?
Incinerator's burning!
Incinerator's burning!
Crash, smash, crunch.
Crash, smash, crunch.

The lonely little teddy,
Climbed up the hill of trash
Looking for a friend
Who hadn't been turned to ash.
An old tin can was there
To brighten up his day,
And the lonely little teddy
Had a friend with whom to play.

Rita and Redmond's
BEST PRANKS

There's nothing Rita and Redmond like better than playing clever tricks on the other Teddy Scares. Read on for Rita and Redmond's most memorable pranks!

Knowing Edwin loves fondue, Rita made him his very own chocolate-dipped treats. When he delightedly bit into one, Edwin quickly realized it wasn't a strawberry—it was a chocolate-covered brussels sprout! *Blech!*

A few days later, Edwin fell for yet another prank: Redmond told Edwin he had baked some brownies, and that they were on a plate near the Incinerator. But when Edwin hurried over to grab one, all he found was a plate full of brown cutouts of the letter E!

Rita had the perfect prank in mind when she found some old clay in the dump. She molded it into a rectangle, wrapped it in a scrap of foil—and offered it to Mazey as a piece of gum. The look on Mazey's snout when she bit into it was priceless!

Thanks to his near-constant naps, Sheldon often finds himself on the receiving end of an R&R prank. One day when he fell asleep, Rita took the opportunity to borrow his hat. While Sheldon napped, she sewed a few extra stitches into it—so that the hat was suddenly two sizes too small! Sheldon was so confused when he woke up and couldn't get his hat back on—it had Rita and Redmond in *stitches* for days!

Rita came up with another prank for Mazey when she found a half-empty bottle of shampoo in a corner of the dump near the Incinerator. Rita squeezed out all of Mazey's toothpaste and refilled the empty tube with the shampoo. When Mazey went to brush her teeth that night, her mouth was full of suds . . . but *not* the kind she had been expecting!

Redmond came up with his own prank to play on Sheldon when he found a few broken alarm clocks around the dump. With Eli's help, Redmond fixed the clocks and set them all to go off at the same time. Then he positioned the alarm clocks near Sheldon's favorite cozy spot for napping. When Sheldon was fast asleep, the alarms all went off at once, giving him a big surprise!

Sheldon Grogg's Top Ten
MIDNIGHT SNACKS

Some nights, the only thing that helps Sheldon settle down for bed is a midnight snack. But his favorite go-to treats all have an a*gore*able twist:

10. Pigs in a blanket: Pieces of bacon or sausage rolled up in scraps of fabric found around the dump.

9. Ants under a log: Not peanut butter with raisins on celery, silly! These are ants that were found under a log.

8. Egg-in-a-hole: An egg served in a cardboard box that has a hole in it.

7. Black-eyed peas and rice: Peas and rice, with some bug eyes tossed on top for crunch.

6. **Sautéed tree ears:** These mushrooms are a type of black fungus that grows in and around the dump.

5. **Mud pie:** A cookie crust filled with chocolate ice cream mixed with mud.

4. **Toad-in-a-hole:** A fried toad served in a cardboard box that has a hole in it.

3. **Ugli fruit:** The most hideously ugly, rotten, and misshapen pieces of fruit you've ever seen.

2. **Strawberry cricket lollipop:** A crunchy cricket encased in sweet strawberry candy.

1. **Grasshopper pie:** A crunchy chocolate cookie with a smooth, green, minty mousse filling, topped with a sprinkle of dried grasshoppers.

TEDDY SCARES MOOD CHART

The Teddy Scares can be a moody bunch. And they can help you keep track of your mood with this chart! Just answer the question: Today I feel . . .

HAPPY

DEPRESSED

SAD

FRUSTRATED

SLEEPY

STUBBORN

ANGRY

GRUMPY

LONELY

PESSIMISTIC

ANNOYED

EXCITED

Sheldon's Lullaby

Sheldon's favorite lullaby will give you *agore*able dreams as you creep it real overnight:

Creepy teddy, lay your head

On this garbage-covered bed.

The Incinerator gleams in the gloom

Onto the Trash Hills under the moon.

Try not to give yourself a fright

As Teddy Scares say goodnight!

Creepy dreams!